CALCULATED DISASTER

MEYARI MCFARLAND

CONTENTS

Special Offer	v
Other Books by Meyari McFarland:	vii
Calculated Disaster	1
Author's Note: Hope in the Dark	10
1. Tired	11
2. Sleep	19
Other Books by Meyari McFarland:	27
Afterword	29
Author Bio	31

SPECIAL OFFER

The rainbow has infinite shades, just as this collection covers the spectrum of fictional possibilities.

From contemporary romances like *The Shores of Twilight Bay* to dark fantasy like *A Lone Red Tree* and out to SF futures in *Child of Spring*, *Iridescent* covers the gamut of time, space and genre.

Meyari McFarland shows her mastery in this first omnibus collection of her short fiction. Twenty-five amazing stories, all with queer characters going on adventures, solving mysteries, and falling in love are here in the first Rainbow Collection.

And now you can get this massive collection of short queer fiction, all of it with the happy endings you love, *for free!*

Sign up here for your free copy of Iridescent now!

OTHER BOOKS BY MEYARI MCFARLAND:

Day Hunt on the Final Oblivion

Day of Joy

Immortal Sky

A New Path

Following the Trail

Crafting Home

Finding a Way

Go Between

Like Arrows of Fate

Out of Disaster

The Shores of Twilight Bay

Coming Together

Following the Beacon

The Solace of Her Clan

You can find these and many other books at www.MDR-Publishing.com. We are a small independent publisher focusing on LGBT content. Please sign up for our mailing list to get regular updates on the latest preorders and new releases and a free ebook!

Copyright ©2024 by Mary Raichle

Print ISBN: 978-1-64309-113-6

Cover image

Deposit Photo ID# 692874206 by Alla Serebrina

All rights reserved. No part of this publication may be reproduced or transmitted in any form or by any means, electronic or mechanical, including photocopy, recording or any information storage and retrieval system, without permission in writing from the publisher.

Requests for permission to make copies of any part of the work should be emailed to publisher@mdr-publishing.com.

This book is also available in TPB format from all major retailers.

❀ Created with Vellum

This story is dedicated to my best friend Kay who's been telling stories with and to me for years now.

CALCULATED DISASTER

"Hey, babe, you looking for heaven? Because I think it's right behind you."

Lei's eyes slid shut as she fought a shudder. Her shoulders sagged. Her hands clenched on the counter hard enough that it creaked. The kitchen was dead-quiet. Cyan had made a little squeaking noise right around "babe" and Arin's breath whistled between her teeth. If Lei looked, she just knew that Arin would be deer-in-the-headlights googly-eyed with horror.

Justified. Totally justified.

Lei breathed in slowly, lips pursed as she made her hands release the counter. Not broken. That was good. The thing was a good fifty years old, orange laminate that should've been catapulted into the sun about the time Lei was born, but then most every fixture in Cyan's apartment was like that.

Old, battered, nearly broken and "vintage" according to her landlord. Asshole.

"Stevie," Lei said.

She turned and looked down, down, down into Stevie Thorsen's bright blue eyes. He was all of about five foot tall, beard only just starting to come in now that he'd finally gotten on T. He'd been an annoying brat before that. He was an annoying brat now.

Stevie grinned up at Lei. "Hey. You're looking fine."

"Those lines are rude as hell," Lei said. She did not cross her arms over her chest because that would just draw Stevie's eyes straight to her boobs and Lei had spent way too much money getting those boobs to share them with Stevie. "They don't work as pickup lines. They just insult people."

"You have absolutely no sense of humor," Stevie said with sigh and a roll of his eyes. "Seriously, it's the holidays. It's a party. Pickup lines are a thing that happens. Besides, I'm not talking about me."

Lei narrowed her eyes. "What."

Stevie's grin went full-on cheesy as he wagged his eyebrows at Lei. "Heaven? Not me. I'm all about the hell. Nope, my second cousin, the one from Missoula? She's in town and she's sweet, kind, gentle, and about as socially adept as I am. Just in the awkward way instead of the cheesy way."

That sent one eyebrow up towards Lei's hairline. At six foot six, there weren't many people in the party who were taller than Lei. No amount of estrogen was going to fix that, of course, but that wouldn't stop Lei from wearing her heels to a party. She had a great view across the entire great room with its ridiculous sunken conversation pit, the big leather sofa that Cyan had insisted on adding when Lei commented on just what a blacklight might show in that pit, and bookshelves along every wall for Cyan's huge collection of books.

No one was reading the books.

Almost no one.

One girl, six foot one or two, in sensible black lesbian shoes with her purple shoulder-length hair pulled into her mouth to chew on, stood in the darkest corner behind the sofa. She'd picked the exact spot where the lights were lowest. Between the sofa and the stupid yellow shag carpet making it sit awkwardly, she was hidden with her book.

Mostly. Not completely. But enough that Lei had to actually look at her to see what she was like and that was enough to make Lei's cheeks go red. Stevie chuckled.

"Shut up."

"You'll like her," Stevie said confidently just as he always did everything. The man was more confident than anyone had any right to be, damn him. "Kamalani Gadhavi, twenty-seven, A positive, Virgo, trans like a quarter of the people here and queer like most everyone else here. She's a poet. And an artist. Watercolor."

"You are such an ass," Lei complained.

"Yep," Stevie agreed. He wagged his eyebrows as Arin groaned and rubbed her forehead. "Come on, I'm good at this. I've been matchmaking since second grade and I'm damn good at it. I'm not saying you'll want to get married or anything. But you'd enjoy talking to her and damn it all, if I leave her alone to try and hook up with someone, she'll stay right in that corner all night and never say a word to anyone. It's ridiculous."

"You're asking us to babysit her," Lei said.

This time she did cross her arms over her chest even though Stevie's eyes flicked straight to her boobs before going up to her face with a too-serious expression that made the discomfort in Lei's belly that much more squirmingly distressing.

"No, I'm asking you to talk to her," Stevie said. "She will *not* talk to anyone else. I barely got her in the door. She wants to. Said so on the way here. She's just not able to make that first move. Lei, you're gorgeous. You're strong. You're talented. You're intimidating as fuck. She can hide behind you and feel safe and chit-chat. I don't care. Just go talk to her, okay?"

When Lei glared down at Stevie, he rolled his eyes and shook his head before marching off to talk to Mohinder who'd decided to wear his favorite sari after all. Lei hadn't seen that when she came in. It looked lovely on him, shimmery purple and gold with accents of yellow and blue that gleamed against his dark skin.

Mohinder groaned and rolled his eyes at whatever pickup line Stevie threw at him, but he also laughed and hugged Stevie so yes, Lei had just been handed babysitting duties.

"She does look like your type," Cyan commented entirely too innocently.

"I could go bring her over," Arin offered with a sly little smile that Lei glowered at, to no effect.

"No." Lei sighed. "Stevie's a jerk but he's not that kind of jerk. If he came to me, there's a reason for it. Probably on both sides."

Cyan patted Lei on the shoulder, smile sympathetic enough that Lei didn't glare at her for the way her lips twitched against a smile. The two of them were going to giggle their heads off the instant Lei left the orange monstrosity of a kitchen, damn it. They were justified, of course, but that didn't stop Lei from being embarrassed about it.

Either way, Kamalani glanced up, eyes skimming across the great room. She jerked when she saw Lei looking at her. Even in the dark corner and from that distance, Lei could see the blush rush over Kamalani's face.

Damn Stevie anyway.

Lei huffed and stalked across the room, dodging groups of friends and acquaintances chatting together about who knew what. A couple of them tried to pull Lei into their conversations for introductions or opinions, but Lei waved them off and continued on her way.

Only to find that Kamalani wasn't in the dark corner anymore.

Lei blinked.

"That's odd. I didn't see her move."

Lei looked around, craning her neck and then standing on her tiptoes for that extra inch of height, as if that would make a huge difference in what she could see. There was no sign of Kamalani in the great room. Arin and Cyan were absolutely giggling, heads together as they whispered to each other. Given that Cyan flatly refused to let people play loud music at her parties, they probably were actually whispering to each other.

Stevie was long-gone, hunting through the second bedroom that Cyan used as an office for someone to destroy with horrible pickup lines, probably.

That left the laundry room and the balcony out in the Puget Sound's inevitable rain, wind and cold.

Lei checked the laundry room, empty, and then huffed as she went out onto the balcony and looked into the darkest corner there. She shook her head.

"You're going to freeze out here and Cyan will be very upset her book got wet," Lei said.

Kamalani squeaked and clutched the book even closer to her chest. She was pressed back against the rough cedar planks of the apartment's siding, eyes wide and face blazingly red even with the cold rain slowly soaking her.

"I'm fine," Kamalani protested.

"Get your butt inside," Lei ordered. "I'm serious about Cyan's book."

Kamalani groaned like an organ that had a busted pipe, sliding through three minor keys before pouting up at Lei. She wasn't much taller than Stevie, maybe five foot three, so it was a long ways up for that pout to travel. No surprise that it lost effectiveness before it hit Lei's face.

"In." Lei pointed.

"You're just as bossy as Stevie said you were," Kamalani grumbled under her breath as she shuffled back into the apartment past Lei.

"Yes, well, he said that I had heaven behind my back and that I'd think you were cute," Lei said. She grabbed a towel off the stack in the pantry next to the washer/dryer unit and passed it to Kamalani. "I've never taken Stevie's word for anything and I'm not about to start now. Someone needs to get through his thick skull that pickup lines are demeaning."

"I know, right?" Kamalani exclaimed.

She dried the book first, then gave a swipe at her hair and arms that left most of the rain still on her. When Lei raised an eyebrow, Kamalani rolled her eyes and did a better job of getting dried off.

Up close, she was adorable. Round-cheeked and sweet-faced, especially when pouting about Lei being bossy, Kamalani had the sort of figure that Lei had wanted when she was a child: round, soft, inviting. Lei was the exact opposite: tall, muscular and never going to pass no matter how much surgery she had or how much estrogen she took.

From the little looks Kamalani threw Lei's way, it didn't matter to her.

Her cheeks were not blushing. No, absolutely not. It was just warm in here compared to outside. That was all.

"Do you always glare at people you rescue from the rain?" Kamalani asked once she was no longer dripping.

"Only when they were idiots and went out in the rain for no good reason," Lei answered.

Kamalani pursed her lips and nodded as if that was valid. And it sort of was. Sort of. Lei fought against a sigh that wanted to come up from her toes. Damn Stevie and his matchmaking anyway.

"Are you even looking to date someone?" Kamalani asked.

Lei snorted a laugh, waving for her to follow Lei back into the party. "Of course. It's hard to find a girlfriend when you look like me."

Kamalani frowned, eyes sweeping from Lei's too-strong jaw down to her expensive bust and then onwards to Lei's beautiful stiletto heels. "You intimidate them? I mean, you're gorgeous. Like a model. How can you have problems getting dates?"

If Stevie had said it, Lei would've immediately discounted it. If Cyan or Arin said it, and they did on a daily basis to make Lei feel better, Lei would assume that it was being nice to a friend. The way Kamalani said it, puzzled, head cocked to the side, blinking rapidly, wasn't at all like the normal reassurances Lei got.

Kamalani sounded serious. Looked like she was truly confused. And she frowned up at Lei, waiting for an explanation.

"That's..." Lei tried to find a way to say nicely that Kamalani didn't need to be kind to Lei's feelings. "Look, I'm aware of my appearances. The jaw, my hands, the throat. I'm not... convincing."

If anything, Kamalani looked even more confused.

"I... okay, then," Kamalani said, shaking her head sharply. "And I thought I had self esteem issues. Look, you're beautiful in the powerful amazon warrior sort of way. It's sexy and no, you're not getting clocked. You're getting drooled over. I'm cute in the stereotypical female way, which is nice because I could never, in a million years, look like you. Exercise is not my friend."

She held Cyan's book to her chest, still staring at Lei like she was a puzzle to figure out.

Lei started to say something, then slowly shut her mouth. When she looked back into the great room, Stevie was grinning as he talked to Cyan and Arin, both of whom were nodding and giggling. Kamalani looked too, rolling her eyes when she spotted Stevie through a break in the crowd.

"He's a sneak," Lei complained.

"Stevie?" Kamalani said with an expression that made Lei's nod a foregone conclusion. "Completely. He swore up and down that I'd have fun once I met you."

"He outright said that he was matchmaking for us," Lei said, glaring across the crowd even though there was no way the Stevie could see her from here.

"He does that," Kamalani said much more flatly while glaring through the crowd despite Stevie being hidden from her point of view. "A lot. I told him to stop it."

"He didn't stop," Lei said, rolling her head to look at Kamalani.

Who truly should not be as lovely as she was. The horrible part was that Lei was fairly certain that they could easily hit it off and become friends. Probably lovers. Kamalani was exactly Lei's type, after all.

"No, he didn't," Kamalani agreed. She snorted. "We should never speak to each other again just to spite him."

"No, we shouldn't do that," Lei said. Her cheeks when hot when Kamalani raised an eyebrow at her. "We shouldn't. That's giving in, too. Just in the opposite way. What we should do is go back over, get some treats, and blandly talk to each other without showing any signs of interest."

Kamalani's eyes lit up. She grinned and bounced on her toes while nodding enthusiastically. God, Lei was so damned doomed. Damn Stevie and his corny pickup lines and matchmaking anyway.

"That's perfect!" Kamalani exclaimed. "It's a deal!"

She headed back into the great room, pausing at the

doorway to look over her shoulder with a wry smile at Lei. The way Kamalani looked at Lei, hopeful and doubting and amused all at the same time, the way she licked her lips, shrugging slightly, sent Lei's stomach into an excited roll.

"Not sure how long I'll be able to keep it bland and not flirtatious," Kamalani admitted in a husky voice that sent a thrill straight through Lei. "You're exactly my type."

She slipped into the crowd, moving through it like a salmon swimming upstream. Lei shut her eyes, pressed her lips together and breathed for a moment. Then she followed Kamalani again. What else could she do?

Stevie was right.

Lei had glimpsed heaven in Kamalani's smile. She'd follow her anywhere now.

Not that she had to let Stevie know that, of course. It wouldn't do to give him encouragement for those terrible pickup lines.

AUTHOR'S NOTE: HOPE IN THE DARK

*C*alculated Disaster is a story of sudden meetings giving you a whole new chance at life and love. It's such a great trope that it's probably no surprise that I have other stories that use that trope, too.

Hope in the Dark is a novel that is all about the sudden, chance encounter that change everything. Rutendo and Yannick aren't much like Lei and Kamalani, except for all the ways they are. Either way, I hope you enjoy the sample!

1. TIRED

Rutendo yawned, jaw cracking hard enough that his shuffling footsteps slowed to a stop. He rubbed his eyes which didn't do a single thing for how they burned. A long day on top of a short night on top of a long week with not enough sleep and way too much to do--he was far too tired to think anymore. He wasn't sure that he could walk without running into the walls at this point. Getting from the parking garage's dark, echoing depths to his apartment on the third floor would be a challenge.

There was always too much to do. Kamala, his boss, always said that Rutendo needed to work smarter, not harder. She normally had a worried frown when she fussed at him over his hours and workload but as far as Rutendo could tell all Kamala did was sit in meetings agreeing with all the other bosses that Rutendo didn't have enough to do. Oh, you can handle this, Ru. You're such a team player, Ru. We really appreciate everything you do, Ru.

"Appreciate it with a pay raise, you jerks," Rutendo grumbled. "At least Kamala tries to get me raises."

Not that she'd succeeded yet.

Thankfully, the parking garage was empty, so no one heard him talking to himself. No, not empty. Plenty of cars. No other people. Just Rutendo shuffling his way from his heat-ticking black Hyundai Accent towards the dinky elevator that always smelled of urine. Despite staying until six tonight, Friday night, he'd only just gotten home at not-quite eight. Two hours of traffic to cross thirty-five miles of the Puget Sound: ridiculous but what else was he going to do?

He couldn't afford to live closer to work. Anything close to Seattle cost three to five times his wages. With the loans he had yet to pay off, and that he might never pay off successfully, Rutendo couldn't afford anything but the more distant suburbs of Everett, miles beyond even Everett's city limits.

He shuffled the rest of the way to the elevator, feet aching, eyes burning, jaw cracking every few steps as he yawned. As much as he wanted to, Rutendo couldn't afford to quit. He needed this job. Between his family's perpetual financial problems and his school debt, Rutendo might as well have been chained to the desk at work literally instead of metaphorically.

The elevator dinged. It did, in fact, stink of urine once the door jerkily slid open. Rutendo sighed and shuffled in, carefully not leaning on anything as he pushed the button for the fourth floor.

His briefcase weighed too much. It kept overbalancing him as he tried not to sway. Rutendo covered his mouth with his hand as the biggest yawn yet forced its way out. Four floors, sixteen steps, fumble with his keys and then he'd be able to drop the stupid briefcase and strip down on his way to bed.

Thank goodness for Fridays; he didn't have to do anything for two whole days.

The elevator binged. He waited two endless seconds for the doors to open, then shuffled sixteen steps to room 404, and fumbled for his keys.

They dropped out of his hand to the floor. Rutendo glared at them for their betrayal before carefully bending over and picking them up with exaggerated care.

"You drunk?"

Rutendo yelped and whirled so hard that he staggered into the doorframe. He stared at the very tall, very broad-shouldered man who was mopping sweat off his face with the hem of his T-shirt while watching Rutendo warily. Not as if he was worried about Rutendo attack him. As sculpted as the man's exposed abs were, he was in no danger of Rutendo harming him. No, it was more like he was worried about Rutendo passing out.

"Ah, no?" Rutendo said. "I don't drink. At all. Just… exhausted. It's been a very long week."

"Oh," the very tall man said. He cocked his head to the side and revealed a lush ponytail of thick blond-streaked brown curls that Rutendo wouldn't have believed. He'd assumed that the hair was gelled down rather than pulled back so tightly that the other man's head had to hurt. "I'm your new neighbor, Yannick. Hope I haven't bothered you with the noise."

Rutendo blinked at him. "…Noise? Um, no. Oh! I'm Rutendo. Sorry. I'm kind of… tired."

Yannick stared back, mouth opening and then shutting with a snap. "Right. Obviously didn't hear. Have a great Friday! I'll just… be getting into the shower."

"Ah, sure?" Rutendo said.

He stared as Yannick unlocked his door, 403, with smooth precision that Rutendo ached to be able to match. Yannick waved, smiled as if he thought he'd done something awkward and strange, that smile that always felt and looked completely plastic when Rutendo did it, and then firmly shut his door.

Music sounded a moment later. Death metal on about eleven or so from the sound of it. Loud but not intrusively so. Rutendo blew out a breath, shook his head and turned back to the nearly insurmountable task of unlocking his own door. He really needed a vacation. Especially if he'd somehow lost his last neighbor and then gained a new one without ever noticing the change.

It took three tries to get the key in the lock and then Rutendo was finally able to shuffle into his apartment. He dropped the keys on the wobbly little table he'd found in the garbage bin three years ago. His briefcase went on the floor by the door next to his shoes which Rutendo gratefully kicked off.

Then he stripped off his navy blazer, his tie, pants, shirt and finally underwear as he hurried to his bed. Rutendo faceplanted in the bed and sighed happily before wiggling his way under the covers at last. Tomorrow there would be things to do. Laundry and groceries and maybe even cleaning up his tiny little one-bed apartment. Wash dishes, that'd be good.

Not today.

The sound of Yannick's death metal filtered into the bedroom. It was a distant roar rather like the ocean with occasional louder thumps or groans or something that Rutendo dismissed even as they jarred him out of his doze.

Unfortunately, the music did jar him awake which gave his stomach a chance to reminded Rutendo that he'd missed lunch today and hadn't bothered to stop for dinner. For that matter, he wasn't sure if he'd had breakfast this morning. Coffee. An apple fritter that'd been in the floppy white box which someone, he had no clue who, had left in the kitchen at the office.

Rutendo's stomach growled louder than Yannick's death metal at twenty.

"Fine, food," Rutendo groaned. He fished around at the side of the bed and found his sweatpants, discarded there last Sunday and not put away. The hoodie he'd tossed over the headboard was still there, too. "Huh. I thought I put that in the laundry basket. Oh, well."

Sweats were better than office clothes. Always. Slippers were way too much work to find so Rutendo shuffled barefooted across his faintly sticky floors into the kitchen to stare blearily into the refrigerator.

"Lovely." Rutendo sighed. "Ketchup. Green olives, three left. And that box of Indian takeout from two months ago. Ramen it is."

His pantry, so-called because it was just a tall half-width cabinet on the side of the kitchen closest the door, was nearly as bare as his refrigerator. He had one packet of ramen, the cheap sort that came in a Styrofoam cup, one packet of ramen, the expensive sort that came in a plastic bowl with sealed packages of noodles and three lovely flavor packets. And a jar of caramel sauce that didn't look to have been touched since he put it in the cabinet who knew how long ago.

"Fancy ramen," Rutendo decided as he leaned against the wall to keep from swaying. He still swayed dramatically as he pulled the fancy ramen out, but he didn't dare grab the pantry door. It was already half-broken and Rutendo had nothing to fix it with.

Fancy ramen in the microwave was easier at any rate. Well, it was easier than putting a kettle on, anyway. Rutendo managed to get the cardboard box off the ramen bowl but peeling the plastic defeated him. The little tab tore free instead of peeling the plastic lid off. He glared at it and grabbed his kitchen scissors from the drawer next to the sink. Two attempts at piercing the plastic later, Rutendo braced the bowl with one hand and shoved much harder with the point of the scissors.

Which bounced off and stabbed into the meat of his thumb.

Blood.

Everywhere.

All over the counter, his ramen bowl, the stupid scissors. And Rutendo, too, as he staggered backwards while staring at the blood spurting from his left thumb.

"That's... an artery," Rutendo said. He grabbed a paper towel, sprawling ten more across his counter because he didn't tear it loose, and jammed it against his thumb. "Oh dear. That's deep. Too deep. Oh my. Now... now what?"

No driving. Not like this. No one he could call other than 911 and they'd probably take ages given how minor this was. Rutendo stood there, swaying, shaking, blood soaking through his paper towel in a distinctly alarming way as he fuzzily wondered if he was just too tired to feel the pain or too numb to know that it hurt yet.

Someone to help?

New neighbor?

New neighbor.

Somehow, Rutendo got his front door open. Blood went everywhere as he did it, but he did get the door open. Then he kicked Yannick's door because knocking meant letting go of his thumb and that would mean more blood everywhere and Rutendo couldn't afford to pay for the hallway to be cleaned as thoroughly as it should be. He'd have to clean his apartment himself. Later.

"Yeah?" Yannick said with a scowl that went abruptly horrified as he took in Rutendo standing on his doorstep. "Holy shit, get in here! What the hell happened?"

"I decided I needed to eat," Rutendo said, stumbling as

Yannick dragged him into his much nicer, much brighter, and very clean apartment. "But I had an accident cutting open the ramen packet. It's um, probably an artery? There were spurts."

"You were... ramen..." Yannick stared at Rutendo for a long moment before shaking his head and pushing Rutendo into his sparklingly clean bathroom. Which had a full paramedic's first aid kit tucked between the beautifully white stand sink and the pristinely clean white toilet.

"It's so clean," Rutendo breathed as Yannick maneuvered him to sit on the toilet, gripping his left hand and its wad of bloody paper towel tightly.

"Took a lot of work to get it there," Yannick agreed. "Rent's cheap but I wasn't sure it was worth it until I cleaned the place to within an inch of its life."

He checked Rutendo's thumb, nodded, and then set to work patching him up as professionally as any doctor. Rutendo stared, blinking repeatedly, at Yannick's lush hair because if he looked at the needle poking into his thumb he was going to pass out. Really, what man had hair that gorgeous? It wasn't fair. Not even a hint of a bald spot on top, too.

"Glad you like it," Yannick said with a grin as he snipped the thread off and then smeared some sort of antibiotic over Rutendo's thumb before thoroughly bandaging his hand. "Ten stitches. You really wangied yourself. You'll need to get to a clinic and get a tetanus shot unless you've had one recently."

"...I'm not sure I've ever had a tetanus shot," Rutendo said thoughtfully. "Was I talking out loud?"

"Yep," Yannick said. He grinned. "You were doing it at your door, too. That's why I thought you were drunk."

"I never drink," Rutendo said automatically. "But I kind of

feel drunk. I'm so tired. And hungry. And now there's blood all over my kitchen and the ramen is ruined."

Yannick sighed. "Come on. Crash on my couch for a little bit. I was just making a late dinner. I'll make some for you, too, then help you back to your apartment."

"I couldn't," Rutendo protested even as he nodded that it was the greatest idea anyone had ever had in the history of ever. Which he hopefully hadn't said out loud.

Yannick's snicker probably meant that Rutendo had said it out loud, but he was just flat too tired to care at this point. There were spots of blood on Yannick's bathroom floor and bits of bloody gauze in the trash. A few spots on the living room floor, too, but Yannick didn't seem to mind.

He just pushed Rutendo down onto the couch which was comfier than any bed Rutendo had slept on. Yannick turned the death metal down a few notches, threw a crocheted red and black blanket over Rutendo before he went to work in the kitchen which was a mirror to Rutendo's little kitchenette.

A clean mirror. Clean floors, counters, fridge, cabinets. The stove might never have been used at all. Rutendo sighed as he curled up under the blanket. He really was going to have to clean his apartment. Later. Not now.

Sleep grabbed Rutendo and pulled him under as Yannick started singing softly with the music. His voice was just the right sort of harsh to make the growly music sound good instead of just raw and defiant. Rutendo smiled as he dropped off.

2. SLEEP

Took all of about three seconds for Yannick's next-door neighbor to fall asleep. Shocking that he hadn't fallen asleep on the doorstep given how wiped he looked. The dude was such a mess. Bags on the bags under his eyes, lush brown skin grey-toned, hair all lanky and greasy. Yannick didn't know what the poor guy did for a living, but he clearly needed a vacation like yesterday.

At least he didn't mind the Die Apokalyptischen Reiter. When his Spotify switched to the next song, it was Elysia and all he did was mumble something as he pulled the afghan up over his head.

Dude seriously needed more sleep if he could sleep thought that lineup.

Yannick shook his head as he set leftover chicken curry to heating in the microwave while stirring up a quick salad out of the spinach, a sliced cucumber and about twenty different herbs he'd bought fresh and stuck into the fridge until he could figure out what to do with them. Some nuts, dried cranberries and a fast vinaigrette made the salad workable even without tomatoes. He didn't have rice to go with the curry but there was prepared cous-cous in the fridge. Nuke that, pour the curry on top, add some bread or something.

Ah, yeah, he had the loaf of 8-Grain he'd gotten at the farmer's market on Thursday. That'd round dinner out nicely. Four slices of that with fresh butter he'd made on Monday and there was a good meal.

Probably the best meal that Rutendo had eaten in ages. The suit he'd been wearing had hung on his body. The bloodstained sweats he was wearing now were just as baggy-loose. Yannick frowned. He let the curry sit in the fridge for a moment as he slipped outside and checked on Rutendo's door.

Not locked, thankfully. Yannick eased the door open to peek. Then he pushed it all the way open to stare around Rutendo's apartment in horror.

Dingy windows that clearly had never been cleaned. Floor was a shade of grey that made Yannick's skin crawl. Kitchen was covered in blood and so nasty-filthy that his breath caught. That was leaving aside the empty pantry door hanging open at a 'this is broken' angle, the rickety recliner that clearly had been pulled out of a dumpster somewhere and the clothes scattered across the floor.

"That boy needs help," Yannick said.

He sighed, grabbed Rutendo's keys from the tiny formerly four-legged but now three-legged table by the front door, and then headed back into his own apartment. Rutendo hadn't moved even as the music swung into Deathchain recorded a bit too loudly compared to everything else in the list.

Yannick cleaned up his floor because his OCD wouldn't let him not. Then he cleaned his bathroom three times for the same reason. Then he went back and got dinner ready, setting it up on the coffee table since he judged that Rutendo wasn't gonna be able to sit up at his little dining table without sleeping for at least twenty to twenty-four hours straight.

"Got you food," Yannick said as he gently shook Rutendo awake.

"Mmfg?" Rutendo mumbled.

He didn't fight against waking up even though he should have. Instead, Rutendo sighed and sat up before he even managed to open his eyes. Once he did get them open, they went way wide open at the food laid out in front of him.

"Um, this is... a lot?" Rutendo said hesitantly enough that Yannick snickered at him.

"Maybe, but that's what I was making for myself so that's what you get," Yannick said. He plopped on the couch next to Rutendo, breath catching at the warmth that Rutendo had left behind. "Eat up. Just so you know, I'm probably going to clean your apartment while you sleep. I've got OCD issues and it's making my skin crawl."

Rutendo frowned at him while slowly chewing a bite of salad as if it was an alien entity that might attempt to take over his mind at any moment.

"Yes, really, OCD," Yannick said in answer to the questions he knew were coming. They always came. "No, not just persnickety, for real diagnosed OCD. I can't really stop myself once I know something's messy."

"Oh," Rutendo said. He took another bite of salad, eating more eagerly this time. "That's good. The salad, not the OCD. Really good. Um, thank you? For the food?"

Yannick grinned. "You're welcome. You don't mind on the cleaning?"

"I was going to have to do it anyway and my hand um, hurts," Rutendo said as if he should be ashamed of admitting that a cut that went deep enough into his thumb to cause artery damage, if incredibly minor, would be painful. "I don't feel right letting you do everything, though. That's... I don't know. Sorry. I'm tired."

"I'd give you something for the pain but as tired as you are, I'm worried that you'd have problems," Yannick said. "Eat. Food and sleep will do you more good than anything else."

Rutendo nodded. He ate like a starving man once he got going. The salad didn't inspire much in the way of yummy noises but the instant he took a bite of the curry sex noises came out. Yannick blushed for it. Even as tired and worn-down as Rutendo was, he was an attractive man. Maybe a little too attractive while making sounds like that.

Surprisingly, Rutendo stayed alert all the way to the end of the meal. He didn't talk. Too focused on the food which he ate like it was the best thing he'd ever eaten. Sad, that. Yannick wasn't a great chef. At all. He tried but that was the best of it.

Far too soon, Rutendo was done eating. He promptly started drooping. Yawning and rubbing his eyes like a little kid, the whole thing. Yannick grinned at him.

"Dude, you can totally lie down and sleep some more if you want," Yannick said after finishing the last of his curry. He mopped up the sauce with the final bite of his toast.

"No, I should... I should help clean my apartment," Rutendo insisted.

Yannick shrugged as he gathered the dishes, rinsed all them three times and then put them in the dishwasher. "Picking up your clothes would certainly help."

"Are you going to..." Rutendo started to ask as he stood and then sagged back down to the couch. He wheezed, head nearly hitting his knees before he slowly pushed himself back upright. Mostly. "Oh. Oh my. Okay, I'm more tired than I thought. Um, are you going to have to clean all of it tonight? You said OCD. I'm assuming that you're serious about needing to do it."

Yannick stared at Rutendo. It'd been six years, three months, eight days since someone took his OCD that calmly. Rutendo blinked at him so blurrily that Yannick laughed. Dude didn't have the brain power to fuss over it. Obviously.

"I do... really need... to clean over there," Yannick said, carefully picking his words. "Pretty clear that they never cleaned between tenants."

"Ah, well, no," Rutendo agreed. His cheeks went red. "I kind of didn't fuss over it. I desperately needed an apartment at the time and this one was cheap. Close to the job I had then, too."

Yannick nodded. "I totally get that. But yeah, I'll want to clean it. Thoroughly. I get stuck on threes. But on a thing like cleaning an entire apartment I've... gotten enough control of the OCD that it's not all at once? I mean, I can do one round, quick, and then if you don't mind come back again later. Or just not do it at all."

His shoulders hunched at the thought of leaving the grime there. The thought of that kind of squalor right next door to him was enough to make his heart pound and his stomach churn up his dinner. Yannick swallowed down the desperate need to tell Rutendo that no, absolutely not, he was not allowed to keep Yannick out.

Which no. That was not his apartment. Not his friend. Not his place to be invading Rutendo's apartment and cleaning the fuck out of it.

Even if it clearly needed to happen.

Rutendo nodded once and nearly toppled himself off the sofa. "That's what I thought. Um, one round tonight would be fine. I'm... I'm way too tired to help, though."

"Bed," Yannick agreed. "Maybe help me pick some of your clothes up but after that, it's bed for you."

Yannick had to help Rutendo stand up. Took an arm around his waist which was painfully thin under the too-big sweats. Had he lost a ton of weight or something? Hopefully he hadn't been terribly sick or something.

The apartment was just as terrible on a second look as on the first. Yannick shuddered and then groaned when Rutendo started snickering at him. Turned out that Rutendo was completely and totally incapable of helping at all. He kept nearly falling flat on his face when he tried to bend over to pick up any of his discarded clothes, so Yannick pushed him into his battered old recliner and picked it all up himself.

Then he stripped bed, remade it properly with nice tight corners though he shuddered over the state of the coverlet which looked as though it'd been pulled out of the same dumpster as the recliner and the rickety old table.

"Okay, you have a bed," Yannick announced only to snort because Rutendo'd fallen asleep in his recliner. "Dude. Dude, your life is a disaster."

As much experience as Yannick had with emergency medical situations, it was a simple thing to heft Rutendo up, propel him into the bedroom and then tuck him into bed still wrapped up in his voluminous sweats. Yannick would have to wash the sheets again because of blood transfer from the sweats but Rutendo was just too damned tired for changing into night clothes.

Wherever they were.

Rutendo barely even mumbled over getting tucked in.

Yannick shook his head and then carried Rutendo's laundry across the hall to his apartment. The washer/dryer unit in his closet was one that he'd insisted on. It looked as though Rutendo hadn't asked for one. There was a separate charge for getting a washer/dryer installed and if Rutendo was as broke as it looked like he was, it would be too much for him.

Once the first load of laundry was going, Yannick gathered up his cleaning supplies and set to work on Rutendo's apartment. Just one round of cleaning. That's all he would do and only in the kitchen/living room area. Maybe the bathroom, too, but not the bedroom. He didn't want to wake Rutendo up when the dude clearly needed the sleep.

Yannick put in his earbuds, put on the cleaning Spotify list he'd created to make sure that he didn't keep cleaning forever, and set to work. One way or the other, Rutendo was going to wake up to a better world than he'd had. Maybe not much better but at least it'd be cleaner.

And maybe, if Yannick was lucky, Rutendo would join him for dinner from time to time. Eating alone was miserably lonely. He couldn't say that Rutendo had been a very good dinner companion, but it was still better than waking up alone, working alone, eating alone and forever sleeping alone.

One less lonely task in the day was very much worth any amount of cleaning.

"And man, Dude, this place needs the cleaning," Yannick muttered as he set to work getting rid of the blood all over Rutendo's kitchen. "Ugh."

The first swipe of his hydrogen peroxide-based cleaner turned the counter from slate grey to off-white. Yannick's soul tied to leave his body. He shuddered, swallowed hard, and pulled on the heavy gloves. One round was not going to do it, not in this kitchen.

So be it.

No one could expect him to suffer through this mess. And no one should have to live in it, damn it. He really would have to question Rutendo once he woke up. Maybe over brunch. If the dude didn't sleep until noon, Yannick would be stunned.

He shuddered. Only question would be if Yannick got any

sleep. The level of cleaning Rutendo's apartment needed kinda suggested that tomorrow it would be Yannick's turn for being too tired to stand up straight.

"Still worth it," Yannick muttered as he committed germ death on a biblical scale all over Rutendo's kitchen. "Ugh! Totally worth it."

Hope in the Dark is now available at all major retailers in ebook and TPB format.

OTHER BOOKS BY MEYARI MCFARLAND:

Day Hunt on the Final Oblivion
Day of Joy
Immortal Sky

A New Path
Following the Trail
Crafting Home
Finding a Way
Go Between
Like Arrows of Fate

Out of Disaster

The Shores of Twilight Bay

Coming Together
Following the Beacon
The Solace of Her Clan

You can find these and many other books at www.MDR-Publishing.com. We are a small independent publisher focusing on LGBT content. Please sign up for our mailing list to get regular updates on the latest preorders and new releases and a free ebook!

AFTERWORD

I absolutely hate going to parties. I've got very little social anxiety (unless I'm talking online and then I'm a mess) but parties are just god-awful in my opinion. You have to stay a certain length of time so that you're not rude. There's all kinds of people that you have to talk to about who knows what. Or, more accurately, that you have to listen talk at you about who knows what while they don't listen to you about whatever you think is interesting.

Much better to stay home and read a book or watch TV in my opinion.

That might, possibly, have come out a bit in this story. Just a touch.

That said, this one makes me grin so wide. I love Lei. She's who I want to be when I grow up. I so identify with Kamalani grabbing a book and hiding in a corner to read. And the two of them coming together makes me wiggle with glee.

Such fun!

If you want more stories like this one, please go sign up for my newsletter on www.MDR-Publishing.com. You'll get updates on whatever I've got coming up, special deals and you can get a free ebook or collection of my short stories. Or you can sign up at my Patreon and get access to my art, writing and whatever's going on creatively in my life.

    Thank you for reading!

Meyari McFarland
    April, 2024
    www.MDR-Publishing.com

AUTHOR BIO

Meyari McFarland has been telling stories since she was a small child. Her stories range from adventures appropriate to children to erotica but they always feature strong characters who do what they think is right no matter what gets in their way.

Meyari has been married for twenty years and has no children or pets. She lives in the Puget Sound, WA and enjoys the fog, rain and cool weather that are typical here. When vacation times come, she and her husband usually go somewhere warm like Hawaii or they go on their own adventures to Japan and other far away countries.

Her life has included jobs ranging from cleaning motel rooms, food service, receptionist, building and editing digital maps, auditing and document control.

MORE FROM MEYARI MCFARLAND

Website:

. . .

MEYARI MCFARLAND

www.MDR-Publishing.com

SOCIAL MEDIA:

Patreon - https://www.patreon.com/meyarimcfarland
Mastodon – https://wandering.shop/@MeyariMcFarland
Pillowfort - https://www.pillowfort.social/Meyari
Facebook - https://www.facebook.com/meyari.mcfarland.5
Pinterest - https://www.pinterest.com/meyarim/

IF YOU ENJOYED THIS STORY, **please leave a comment on your favorite site. Also, please sign up for the newsletter so that you can hear about the latest preorders and new releases.**

www.ingramcontent.com/pod-product-compliance
Lightning Source LLC
LaVergne TN
LVHW042004060526
838200LV00041B/1873